DISNEY'S
THE 🐚 LITTLE
MERMAID

Flounder to the Rescue

Bettina Ling

Disney
PRESS

New York

Printed in the United States of America.

First Edition
1 3 5 7 9 10 8 6 4 2

The text for this book is set in 16-point Berkeley Book.

Library of Congress Catalog Card Number: 97-65660

ISBN: 0-7868-4139-7

Contents

CHAPTER ONE

EXPLORING
A SHIPWRECK

Have you ever been called a scaredy-cat or a baby? Ever had someone say you're chicken? Well then, you know how I feel. My name is Flounder, and sometimes my friends call me a guppy because I scare easily.

Oh, don't get me wrong. Life under the sea is great, especially when I'm with my best friend, Ariel.

Ariel is a mermaid. She has six sisters, and they live with their father in Atlantia. Ariel's father, King Triton, is the ruler.

I love goofing around with Ariel. But the thing Ariel likes to do best is look for stuff from the human world. I don't think human junk is so great. Oh, some of it's kind of cool-looking. But we never know what it's used for, so we can't really do anything with it, you know?

Ariel also likes to go above the surface of the ocean to look for real humans. King Triton says humans are dangerous, but Ariel doesn't believe him.

One morning Ariel told me that she'd discovered a shipwreck and wanted to show it to me. Ariel is a really fast swimmer and, as usual, got to the wreck way ahead of me.

"You know I can't swim that fast, Ariel," I panted, swimming up to the shipwreck.

Ariel just smiled at

me and pointed to the ship. "There it is."

I looked at the shipwreck. This was about the hundredth one we'd found, and they all looked the same to me. I think ship-wrecks are scary. They've got lots of dark, creepy corners where anything can hide.

Ariel and I peeked through the portholes of the ship.

"Isn't this ship fantastic?" she said.

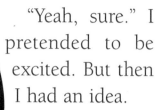

"Yeah, sure." I pretended to be excited. But then I had an idea.

"It looks damp in there." I faked a cough. "And I think I may be coming down with something." I coughed harder.

But Ariel was already starting into the ship. "I'm going inside," she said, swimming through a porthole. "You can stay here and watch for sharks."

"Sharks!" Watching for them was definitely *not* what I wanted to do. "Ariel, wait!"

I started to swim through the porthole, but my head got stuck. "Ariel, help!" I yelled.

"Oh, Flounder," Ariel laughed as she swam back to free me.

I didn't think it was so funny. "Ariel," I whispered, "do you really think there *are* sharks around here?"

"Flounder, don't be such a guppy," she said.

"I'm not a guppy!" I yelled as Ariel pulled me out. I'd show her I was brave. "This is great! I love this!" I said. But I stayed close to Ariel as we explored the ship.

We swam up through a hole in the ceiling to the next level of the ship. On the floor was all kinds of old stuff.

"Oh, my gosh!" Ariel gasped, picking up something small and shiny. "Flounder," she sighed, "have you ever seen anything so wonderful in your life?"

"Wow! Cool!" I said. It *was* neat-looking. Sort of. "What is it?" I asked.

"I don't know," Ariel said. "But I bet Scuttle will!" Scuttle the seagull always told us what the human things were.

I heard a sound nearby. "What was that noise?" I asked Ariel. Ariel was barely listening to me because she was busy picking up yet another human thing.

"Flounder, relax. Nothing's going to happen," she answered calmly.

Just as she said that, there was a crash. A giant shark burst through the ship's porthole. His huge jaws were open and I could see his razor-sharp teeth.

"Shark!" I shrieked, "Ariel, swim!" The shark swam right for me, but I raced away just as his jaws clamped shut. I felt the water ripple behind me.

The shark chased us up to the next floor. Ariel's bag got stuck on a broken plank, but she freed it just as the shark came chomping through the floorboards. We raced on. This was like a bad dream. Only this one was real!

I was so scared that I tried to swim out one of the portholes, but my head got caught again. Ariel pushed me through and the shark charged after us.

We swam up and around the tall mast of the sunken ship. The shark was so close that I panicked, and *Bam!* I banged into the mast.

I started to sink down toward the ocean floor. But Ariel reached through the ring of a big anchor and grabbed me just in time.

The shark was concentrating so hard on catching us that he swam straight into the big anchor ring. His neck stuck tight. I breathed a huge sigh of relief. That'd teach him to chase us! He wriggled angrily, but the ring held fast.

Feeling braver, I stuck out my tongue at the shark. "You big bully!" I said. He snapped his jaws and growled at me. I swam and hid behind Ariel.

"Flounder, you really are a guppy," Ariel laughed as we swam up toward the surface of the water.

"I am not!" How could she say that after I had just fought off a shark? All right, maybe not fought off. But I managed to get away. That was still pretty daring!

Ariel and I surfaced in the middle of the ocean. We spotted Scuttle sitting on a rock and we swam toward him.

"Scuttle!" Ariel called. "Look what we found!"

We showed him the shiny three-pronged object.

"Wow! This is special. Very unusual!" he said.

"What is it?" Ariel asked.

"It's a dinglehopper!" Scuttle replied. "Humans use these little babies to straighten their hair." He showed us by twirling the three-pronged object in his head feathers.

"A dinglehopper," Ariel repeated. "What about this one?" she asked as she held up a wooden tube.

"This I haven't seen in years!" Scuttle said, taking it. "It's a banded, bulbous snarfblatt."

I was impressed. Scuttle sure knew a lot.

"It dates back to prehysterical times when humans used to sit around and stare at each other all day," he continued. "It got very boring, so they invented this snarfblatt to make fine music." He took a deep breath and blew into the wooden tube. Seaweed and water gushed out the top.

I thought that humans sounded weird, sitting around all day staring at each other and straightening their hair.

Suddenly Ariel gasped. "Music! The concert!" she cried. "Oh, my gosh! I'm late! My father's going to kill me."

"The concert was today?" I exclaimed. Ariel and her sisters were supposed to perform for the whole kingdom today. Ariel was a great singer, and everybody in Atlantia was coming to hear her. King Triton had been talking about it all week.

Ariel stuffed the human junk in her bag. "I'm sorry. We've got to go. Thanks, Scuttle!"

We dove beneath the surface. Ariel not showing up for the concert meant big trouble!

CHAPTER TWO

FACING THE MUSIC

Oh, man, King Triton was one angry king! I waited outside the throne room and listened as he yelled at Ariel for missing the concert.

"I just don't know what we're going to do with you, young lady," the king said. "As a result of your careless behavior, the entire celebration was—"

"Ruined!" I heard the voice of Sebastian, the court composer. Normally, we were all friends, but Ariel's missing the concert had made him as mad as the king. "Thanks to you," Sebastian said, "I am the laughingstock of the entire kingdom!"

I hated to hear Ariel being yelled at and getting all the blame. Even though the king

scared me, I still couldn't let Ariel be blamed for everything. Before I could stop to think, I swam into the throne room. "It wasn't her fault!" I cried. "First this shark chased us—"

Both Sebastian and the king stopped yelling and stared at me. That made me *very* nervous, but I continued anyway. ". . . And we tried to . . . and . . . we . . . *grrr*," I said, baring my teeth. I shook my head back and forth, acting as mean as I could. "And then there was this seagull, and—"

"Seagull!" King Triton roared.

Whoops! I covered my mouth. I'd just stuck my fin in it.

"You went up to the surface again, didn't you?" King Triton yelled, his face bright red. Now I was very scared. I hid behind Ariel.

"How many times must we go through this! You could have been seen by one of those barbarians, those humans!"

"They're not barbarians!" Ariel said.

"They're dangerous!" the king cried.

"I'm sixteen years old," Ariel said angrily. "I'm not a child anymore, Daddy!"

"Don't you take that tone of voice with me, young lady," the king shouted. "As long as you live under my ocean, you'll observe my rules!"

"But if you would only listen—"

"Not another word! You are never to go to the surface again! Is that clear?"

I peeked at Ariel. Oh, no! She was staring boldly at her father, ready to start arguing with him again. I did not want her to do that. You have no idea how scary the king is when he's mad.

But then Ariel's lip started trembling and she got tears in her eyes. She turned and swam out of the throne room. I breathed a sigh of relief as I followed her.

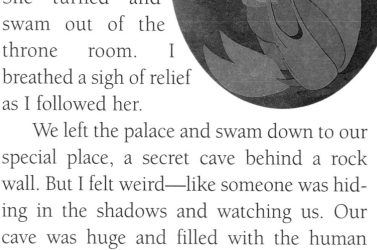

We left the palace and swam down to our special place, a secret cave behind a rock wall. But I felt weird—like someone was hiding in the shadows and watching us. Our cave was huge and filled with the human stuff that we'd collected.

"Ariel, are you okay?" I asked.

"Oh, Flounder," Ariel sighed. "If only I could make Father understand. I don't see how a world that makes such wonderful things could be so bad." She touched one of her human treasures. "What I wouldn't give

13

to see what the human world is like!"

I have to admit, I didn't share Ariel's desire to see the human world. And I didn't completely disagree with the king—about humans being dangerous, I mean. Since Ariel and I had never actually met a human, I did think the king could be right. And I would just as soon not have to find out.

All of a sudden, there was a crash. Sebastian had followed us to the cave and he looked really mad. I ran and hid. Sebastian scared me when he was angry almost as much as the king!

"Sebastian!" Ariel cried.

"Ariel, what is all this?" Sebastian yelled.

"It's just my collection," Ariel replied.

"If your father knew about this place, he'd—"

"You're not going to tell him, are you?" I asked. If the king knew that Ariel was collecting human stuff he'd really go off the deep end.

"Oh, please, Sebastian," Ariel pleaded.

"He would never understand."

Sebastian took Ariel's hand and began pulling her toward the cave's entrance. "Come with me, Princess," he said. "I'll take you home and get you something warm to drink."

I felt a large shadow pass over us. I looked up to the small cave opening, way above our heads.

"What do you suppose that is?" Ariel murmured. She slipped out of Sebastian's grip and swam upward.

I couldn't believe it! After everything the king had said to her, Ariel was heading for the surface again! She was going to get us in more trouble for sure.

"Ariel!" Sebastian called. We raced after her.

CHAPTER THREE

HUMANS!

When we got to the surface I forgot about everything else! A large ship sat in the water. Bright, colorful lights burst from the ship. They lit up the night sky with a huge bang, then floated down into the water.

I looked over at Ariel. I could see she was just as excited as I was. She started swimming toward the ship.

When we caught up with her, Ariel was peeking through an opening in the side of the ship. I looked up to see what was happening on board. Creatures that looked like

Ariel but had two long things instead of a fish tail were dancing around, laughing and singing. They must be humans, I realized. And those long things were their legs!

I spotted a slobbery, furry creature with four legs. It made barking sounds like a seal. When the creature saw Ariel, it ran over and licked her face.

"Max!" a voice called. "Here, boy!"

The creature named Max ran over to one of the humans. It jumped up and put its two front legs on the man's chest. The human laughed. He had dark hair and held a reed-like instrument.

I heard a noise behind us and turned to see Scuttle flapping his way down next to Ariel. "Hey there, sweetie!" he called loudly. "Quite a show!"

"Be quiet, they'll hear you!" Ariel said, grabbing Scuttle's beak. "I've never seen a human this close before. He's very handsome, isn't he?" Ariel was staring at the man with the dark hair like she was in a trance. I'd never seen Ariel look at anyone this way before.

An older human began shouting, "Silence!" He stood by something large.

"It is now my honor and privilege to present Prince Eric with a very special birthday present," the old guy announced. The other humans cheered.

So the human that Ariel thought was so special was called Prince Eric. The prince

turned red and said to the old guy, "Aw, Grimsby, you old beanpole, you shouldn't have!"

Grimsby pulled off a canvas sheet.

Underneath was a statue of Eric holding a sword in his hand and looking like he'd just won a battle or something.

Grimsby and the other humans looked pleased, but I thought Eric seemed embarrassed. "Gee, Grim, it's really something."

"Well, I had hoped it would be a wedding present, but . . ."

Eric chuckled. "Come on, Grim, don't start that again."

"Oh, Eric," Grimsby said. "The entire kingdom wants to see you happily settled down with the right girl."

Eric walked to the railing and looked out to sea. "Oh, she's out there somewhere. When I find her, I'll know."

I looked at Ariel, who was still staring at Eric. She really thought this guy was Mr. Fantastic.

All of a sudden, there was the sound of thunder. Lightning flashed through the sky. I hated being above the water in a storm. Lightning scared me.

"Hurricane a-coming!" a man shouted. "Secure the rigging!"

The other humans started tying down the sails and ropes. A huge wave rose above the ship. It crashed over Ariel's head. Sebastian and I were swept up in the wave and thrown underwater.

I struggled back up toward the surface.

A crack of lightning struck the ship and the big sail caught fire. The flames spread. Eric was trying to guide the ship away from the rocks.

It was too late. *Wham!* The ship

crashed and humans went flying across the deck. Eric and Grimsby  fell overboard. They landed near a small lifeboat. Eric jumped aboard and pulled Grimsby in.

Another wave crashed against me. I struggled to keep on the surface. Then I heard a bark coming from the fiery ship. Max was still on it! Eric dove from the small boat and swam toward the burning ship.

"Max!" Eric called, pulling himself up on deck. Just then, the huge burning mast above Eric broke and fell. Flames were everywhere. Max jumped into Eric's arms, and Eric ran to the railing. But then, Eric's foot broke through the wooden deck and he got stuck! Eric tossed Max overboard. But before Eric could pull his foot out, there was a loud boom. A huge explosion blew up the ship and knocked me under the water!

CHAPTER FOUR

ARIEL IN LOVE

I swam back up. Chunks of wood and metal from the destroyed ship were falling everywhere. I looked for Sebastian or Ariel. But the rainstorm and high waves made it hard to see.

Finally I saw Ariel a few feet away. Then

I spotted Eric, barely on the water's surface, unconscious. Ariel saw him, too, and swam over to him. She wrapped her arms around him, lifted his head above the water, and headed toward the shore.

I tried to follow, but the waves tossed me up and down. Even for a fish, it was hard swimming. I was really scared. Could a fish drown? Sebastian surfaced near me.

A huge wave carried us to a rock near the shore. When I looked at the beach I saw Ariel sitting by Eric. He'd regained consciousness and was staring up at Ariel as she sang to him. She was allowing this human to *see* her!

Max and Grimsby appeared down the beach. Ariel quickly jumped into the water and hid by our rock.

Eric was shaking his head as if trying to clear it. "A girl rescued me . . . ," he mumbled. "She . . . she was singing. She had the most beautiful voice!"

Grimsby pulled Eric to his feet. "Eric, I think you've swallowed a bit too much seawater. Come on now, off we go!"

Eric and Grimsby walked up the beach.

"We are going to forget this whole thing ever happened!" Sebastian said nervously. "The Sea King will never know. You won't tell him." I nodded in agreement. You bet I wouldn't!

Ariel wasn't listening. She was still looking at Eric. She watched until Eric and Grimsby had disappeared out of sight.

Sebastian and Ariel swam back to Atlantia, but I wanted to be alone for awhile. I took my time swimming back to the palace. This whole day had been way too exciting for me. First we got chased by a shark, then the king yelled at Ariel, then we met humans, and the storm and explosion and . . . I wanted to go back to just goofing around.

As I swam along I came across the statue of Eric from the ship. It had sunk to the ocean floor after the explosion. I decided maybe if Ariel had the statue she'd be happy and could forget about going back up to the surface to find the human. I got a bunch of my fish friends to help me drag it to the secret cave, and then I went to get Ariel.

I couldn't wait for Ariel to see the statue. "Come on!" I called as I led her into the cave.

"Flounder, why can't you tell me what this is about?" Ariel pleaded.

"You'll see. It's a surprise!"

Ariel stopped and put her hands over her heart when she saw the statue of Eric.

"Oh, Flounder, you're the best!" Ariel exclaimed. "It looks just like him. It even has his eyes!"

She happily floated around the statue. Maybe this would work. She'd be content with her Eric statue and forget going back to the surface.

Suddenly I noticed Sebastian in the cave entrance. Next to him was King Triton!

"Daddy!" Ariel cried when she saw her father.

King Triton stepped out of the entrance and into the cave. He was angry. Oh, man. This was not good, not good at all. I hid behind a chest, shaking with fear.

"I set certain rules, and I expect those rules to be obeyed," King Triton said. "Is it true you rescued a human from drowning?"

The king somehow knew about Eric! This was terrible!

"Daddy, I had to!" Ariel protested.

"Contact between the human world and the merworld is strictly forbidden. Ariel, you know that!"

"He would have died!"

"One less human to worry about!" King Triton scowled.

"Daddy, I love him!"

Ariel gasped and put her hands to her mouth. I stared in horror. I couldn't believe Ariel had just said that to her father.

King Triton's jaw dropped in shock. "No! Have you lost your senses completely? He's a human, you're a mermaid!"

"I don't care!" she replied.

"So help me, Ariel, I have to get through to you," the king said forcefully. "And this seems to be the only way!"

King Triton pointed his trident at Ariel's collection of human things. I cringed as a beam of orange light shot from the trident and zapped one of Ariel's treasures to bits.

"Daddy! No!" Ariel screamed. "Stop it! Stop it!"

But King Triton zapped object after object until everything was destroyed. Then he pointed his trident at the statue of Eric, and it exploded into tiny pieces.

"Daaaddy!" Ariel screamed.

The king gave Ariel another harsh look before his trident stopped glowing. I sighed with relief.

The statue was now only a pile of jagged stones. Ariel put her head down and began to cry.

The king suddenly seemed sad about his daughter's unhappiness, but he left the cave without saying anything. Sebastian and I came out of our hiding places.

"Ariel," Sebastian said softly. "I—"

"Just go away," Ariel replied.

Quietly, Sebastian and I swam out of the cave and waited near the entrance.

I felt so bad. All of Ariel's human treasures were destroyed. I didn't want to be a baby, but I just couldn't help myself. I started to cry. "Poor Ariel," I sobbed.

"I didn't mean to tell," said Sebastian. "It was an accident." Sebastian explained that he'd mistakenly told the king about Eric.

Suddenly I heard voices inside the cave. Someone was talking to Ariel. I glanced up and saw Ariel swimming off, following two creepy-looking eels. Flotsam and Jetsam!

"Ariel!" Sebastian gasped. "Where are you going! What are you doing with this riffraff?"

"I'm going to see Ursula," Ariel retorted.

"Ariel, no!" Sebastian said. "She's a demon!"

Ariel was going to see the Sea Witch!

Ariel gave Sebastian a disgusted look.

"Why don't you go tell my father!" she taunted. "You're good at that!" Then she swam away.

This was not the Ariel that I knew and loved. She wasn't acting like herself. To go see the meanest, nastiest creature in the ocean? What could she be thinking! The idea of Ariel going to Ursula's awful cave terrified me. Someone had to protect her. As scared as I was of Ursula, I still had to go with Ariel. I looked at Sebastian to see if he thought the same thing.

"Come on," he waved at me. We hurried after Ariel.

CHAPTER FIVE

A DEADLY DEAL

You know how you can imagine that something you've never seen is really horrible? And then you finally see it and find out it's not as scary as you thought? Ursula's cave turned out to be *as awful* as I thought it would be. Even worse.

Sebastian and I hid outside the entrance as Flotsam and Jetsam led Ariel into the cave. At the entrance there was a disgusting bunch of slimy, lumpy creatures with sad eyes.

"Come in, my child," a deep voice called. Ursula was sitting on a giant shell. Boy, she was a huge blob! I'd never seen such an evil face before. And her long black tentacles looked really dangerous.

"Now then," Ursula slid across the seafloor, "you're here because you have a thing for this human, this prince fellow. Well, the only way to get what you want is to become a human yourself."

"Can you change me into one?" Ariel asked.

"My dear sweet child, that's what I do." Ursula circled around Ariel. "Help unfortunate merfolk like yourself." She waved her arms over a giant pot-shaped shell. Creepy ghostlike figures of a sad-looking merman and an ugly mermaid rose from the pot.

"They come to me," Ursula continued, "and for a price, I grant their wishes." She snapped her fingers. The spirit figures turned into happy and beautiful merpeople.

"Of course, once in a while someone can't pay the price." Ursula looked at the two ghostly figures and made a fist. Instantly the figures were pulled into the pot and changed into lumps like the gross creatures by the cave entrance.

"Here's the deal," Ursula said. "I will make you a potion that will turn you into a human for three days."

I didn't like what I was hearing. Ursula proposing a deal to Ariel was bad, very bad. Sebastian and I swam into the cave.

"You must get dear old Princie to fall in love with you and give you the kiss of true love," Ursula was saying. "If he kisses you before the sun sets on the third day, you'll remain human permanently. But if he

doesn't, you turn back into a mermaid—and you belong to me!"

"No, Ari—," Sebastian started to scream, but Flotsam quickly wrapped himself around Sebastian's mouth. Then Jetsam grabbed me. I struggled to get away, but the eel was too strong.

"There is one more thing," Ursula said. "The subject of payment."

"But I don't have anything!" Ariel said.

"I'm not asking much. You'll never even miss it," Ursula smiled. "What I want from you is your voice."

I watched in fright as pinkish smoke

began to rise from Ursula's magic pot. In the middle of the smoke Eric's face began to form. Ariel stared at it.

"Just sign this scroll and we have a deal," Ursula said. She flicked her wrist, and a large golden scroll magically appeared. It said:

I hereby grant unto Ursula, the Witch of the Sea, one voice, for all eternity.

Signed, —————————— .

A fish-skeleton pen appeared above Ariel's head. "Go ahead," Ursula said. "Sign."

"No, Ariel!" I struggled with Jetsam but it was no use. Ariel signed her name.

Ursula grabbed the scroll and triumphantly held it up. The scroll disappeared in a burst of light. Flotsam and Jetsam let go of Sebastian and me. Ursula waved her arms over the pot, chanting a magic spell. Two green, smoky hands rose up from the pot. "Now sing!" Ursula commanded Ariel.

Ariel obeyed, and as she sang, the green, smoky hands pulled her voice from her throat and turned it into a glowing light. Ursula held up a seashell locket that hung around her neck. The hands placed the singing light inside it. With a wave of Ursula's fat hand, Ariel's tail was gone. She now had two legs!

Ariel struggled to swim, but she was not used to her legs. And she couldn't breathe! She was a human now, and she was drowning! Sebastian and I grabbed Ariel and raced with her toward the surface.

We pushed Ariel up through the water. She took a big gulp of air. But she was so weak we had to tow her to shore. Scuttle joined us, and we watched as Ariel tried to stand on her new legs.

"Ariel's got to make the prince fall in love with her," I told him. "He's got to kiss her."

"And she's only got three days!" Sebastian added.

Scuttle made Ariel some human clothes from a white sail and rope he'd pulled off a nearby shipwreck.

Now we had to figure out a way for Ariel to meet Eric.

CHAPTER SIX

AT THE PALACE

Suddenly I heard barking. Max came bounding over a sand dune with Eric close behind! How perfect! The prince came to us! Ariel's smile grew bigger when she saw Eric.

"Max, quiet!" Eric said, as Max barked excitedly. "What's gotten into you, fella?" Eric spotted Ariel. "Are you okay, miss?" he asked. "I'm sorry if Max scared you. He's really harmless."

Ariel smiled and blushed.

"You seem familiar to me," Eric said. "Have we met?"

Max got behind Eric and pushed him closer to Ariel. "We have met!" he said, taking Ariel's hands. "You're the one I've been looking for! What's your name?"

Ariel opened her mouth, but no sound came out.

"What is it?" Eric asked. "You can't speak!"

Sadly Ariel shook her head.

"Oh, then you can't be who I thought," Eric said, sounding disappointed.

Ariel slipped from her rock and fell right into Eric's arms.

"Whoa, careful!" Eric clutched her tightly. "Gee, you must have really been through something. Don't worry, I'll help you. Come on." Eric helped her walk. This seemed to be going better than expected. Eric was taking Ariel to his palace! I was sure he'd fall in love with her!

Sebastian hid in a fold of Ariel's dress so he could go with her. Scuttle and I waved and wished her good luck. I crossed my fins and hoped I'd hear from Sebastian that Ariel had indeed gotten Eric to give her the kiss of true love.

Early the next morning, Sebastian came back to the shore to let us know that Eric and Ariel were going to take a carriage ride and tour the kingdom. There'd been no kiss yet, but it was looking good. This ride could present some great chances for the big kiss.

Well, Ariel and Eric rode around all day. They stopped at a country fair, had a picnic, and danced. Eric bought her flowers and a new hat. He even let her drive the carriage. But he didn't kiss her. Boy, this guy was slow!

That night, Eric took Ariel on a rowboat ride across the lagoon. The setting was very romantic. Now, I thought, he'll kiss her for sure. I was getting worried. Ariel's time was getting shorter.

Eric and Ariel were just drifting along in the boat, so Sebastian took matters into his own hands. He got some romantic music going and helped Eric guess Ariel's name. Finally, Eric leaned closer to Ariel, his lips puckered up, ready to kiss. I flipped my tail

with excitement. This was it!

Suddenly the rowboat flipped over, dumping Ariel and Eric into the water. The romantic mood was broken. I couldn't believe it! We'd have to figure out another way to get Eric to kiss her. They'd come so close, though, I was sure we'd come up with a plan in time.

But late the next afternoon, I found Ariel and Sebastian down at the royal dock. Ariel was slumped against a pillar, her eyes filled with tears. I knew something bad had happened. Sebastian told me that the prince was getting married that day! And it wasn't to Ariel, but to some girl named Vanessa!

I was stunned! This was a complete mess. From the dock, we watched Eric's wedding ship, filled with guests, sail out to sea. Ariel had not been invited. She buried her head in her arms and sobbed. I felt so bad for her that I started to cry, too.

Then Scuttle came swooping down.

"Ariel!" he said, flustered and out of breath. "On the ship, I saw the watch—the witch! Do you hear what I'm saying? The prince is marrying the Sea Witch in disguise!"

"Are you sure?" Sebastian said, as Ariel sat up.

So that was it! Vanessa was actually Ursula, the Sea Witch! She must have put Eric under a spell. "What are we going to do?" I cried. This was the third day and the sun would be setting soon. Ariel's time was almost up. She had to kiss Eric before sunset.

Ariel dove into the water. But she started splashing around helplessly, because she'd forgotten that she didn't know how to swim with legs. Sebastian cut the string that held a row of barrels together, and they splashed

into the water. "Ariel, grab on to one of them!" he called. "Flounder, take the rope and pull Ariel to the boat! I've got to get to the Sea King. He must know about this."

"What about me?" Scuttle pleaded.

"Find a way to stall that wedding!"

CHAPTER SEVEN

FRIENDS TO THE RESCUE

I tugged the barrel carrying Ariel. Scuttle called to all his buddies in the area to come help us. Bluebirds, flamingos, ducks, seals, dolphins, starfish, and lobsters all followed him to the wedding ship.

As Ariel and I neared the ship, I heard the wedding music begin. Vanessa and Eric were walking down the center of the boat together. The seashell necklace around Vanessa's neck glowed brightly. I glanced at the sunset. The bottom of the sun was now just touching the horizon. We'd have to hurry. "Don't worry, Ariel. We're going to make it," I said, pulling harder.

The wedding ceremony started. "Do you,

Eric, take Vanessa to be your lawfully wedded wife for as long as you both shall live?" a guy in a long white robe said.

Eric stared, in a trance. "I do," he said.

"And do you, Vanessa—"

Suddenly I heard screeching and squawking over my head. I looked up. Yes!

The birds that Scuttle had called for help were diving toward Vanessa! She covered her head with her hands as Scuttle and the birds swooped down. "Oww!" she shrieked.

The wedding party ran in all directions.

Ariel and I reached the ship, and she started to climb up. Scuttle's friends launched a full attack on Vanessa, dumping water on her and biting and pinching her. Some seals heaved Vanessa across the deck and into the wedding cake.

Ariel got on board just as Vanessa struggled out of the wedding cake. The sun was almost below the water. Only a few more minutes and the day would be over! Scuttle lunged forward and clamped his beak around Vanessa's seashell locket. "Why, you little—," Vanessa said, grabbing his neck. She started choking him. I heard a bark and saw Max running toward Vanessa. He sank his teeth into Vanessa's rear end. All right!

Vanessa screamed and let go of Scuttle. He fell to the deck, dropping the locket. It crashed to the deck and broke. The golden mist containing Ariel's voice rose from the shell. Her voice began to sing as the mist swirled right into Ariel's throat. She opened her mouth and her singing rang out over all the noise.

Eric came out of his trance. "Ariel?" he asked, his voice a hoarse whisper.

"Eric," Ariel said. She could speak again!

"You can talk!" Eric said. "You *are* the one!"

"Eric, get away from her!" Vanessa shouted, looking desperately at the setting sun.

Eric didn't seem to hear Vanessa. He started to kiss Ariel.

Finally, I thought, glancing at the sunset. Just in time.

"Eric, no!" Vanessa cried out, and Eric paused for a split second. The sun slipped below the water.

Ariel suddenly stiffened as if in pain. "Oh!" she gasped. She slumped to the deck, and Eric caught her. He was staring at Ariel's legs. But they weren't legs anymore. Her tail had returned! After all we'd done, it was too late.

Vanessa screamed in triumph and raised her arms over her head. Bolts of lightning shot out of her hands as she turned back into her real self, fat and ugly. She grabbed Ariel and sneered at Eric. "So long, loverboy!" she screeched. Holding Ariel, she slithered over the railing. Ariel was dragged into the sea.

I dived below the surface of the water and followed Ursula and Ariel downward. I saw Flotsam and Jetsam swimming behind them. I knew the Sea Witch was taking Ariel to her underwater cave. I wasn't scared anymore. I was mad, and I was not going to let that evil blubber-woman hurt my friend.

I heard a shout. "URSULA! STOP!" In front of Ursula stood King Triton, holding his glowing trident. Sebastian floated nearby. He'd managed to find the king.

"Let her go!" he commanded.

Ursula reached forward and gave the king a shove. "Not a chance, Triton! She's mine now!" With a blast of Ursula's magic, the scroll appeared from one of her tentacles. "We made a deal!"

Flotsam and Jetsam wrapped their tails around Ariel's arms, holding her prisoner. "Daddy, I'm sorry," Ariel cried.

Ursula held the scroll up in front of King

Triton's face. The king tried to destroy the contract with a blast from his trident. But the trident had no effect! I started to feel afraid again. Maybe the king wasn't as powerful as Ursula.

"You see," Ursula said, as the king read the scroll, "the contract is legal, binding, and completely unbreakable." She grabbed the scroll and threw it over her shoulder. It dissolved into a golden swirl and circled around Ariel, trapping her. I watched in terror as she began to shrink and turn into one of the souls in Ursula's collection! I felt helpless. I couldn't do anything for my friend.

King Triton's eyes were wide with horror. That fat witch gave him a sly smile. "Of course, I might be willing to make an exchange—for someone even better!"

King Triton stared at Ariel with sorrow in his eyes. He pointed his trident toward the scroll. It sent out a blast of gold light, changing Ariel's signature to his. The king had exchanged himself for Ariel!

Blubber-babe threw back her head with laughter. "It's done!"

Inside the golden swirl, Ariel grew to normal size. The swirl settled around the king. "No!" Ariel screamed.

Slowly King Triton shrank. His crown fell to the ground. In seconds all that was left of him was a small shaking lump with sad yellow eyes.

I stared in shocked silence at the once mighty king. We'd lost and Ursula had won!

Ursula snatched the crown and put it on. "At last it's mine!" She grabbed the trident with one of her tentacles.

I heard an angry sound come from Ariel. She was looking at Ursula, and her face was filled with hate. "You monster!"

Ariel's anger made me start to feel brave again. But then Ursula pointed the trident at Ariel. "Don't fool with me! Contract or no, I'll blast—," Ursula screamed as suddenly a harpoon ripped through one of her arms. Prince Eric was swimming above her.

"Eric!" Ariel called out.

"Why, you little fool!" Ursula shouted up at him. "After him!" she ordered Flotsam and Jetsam.

Eric swam upward and burst through the surface. Flotsam and Jetsam pulled him back under.

Seeing those yucky eels trying to drown Eric made me mad. I found courage inside I never knew I had. I looked over at Sebastian. "Come on!" he shouted. We raced toward Eric. Sebastian pinched Flotsam as hard as he could. I gave Jetsam a good slap in the face with my tail. The eels let go of Eric, but Ursula aimed the trident at him.

Ariel grabbed Ursula's hair and pulled. Screaming in pain, Ursula jerked backward. The trident's ray went off course—and hit Flotsam and Jetsam, destroying them.

Ariel and I swam to the surface.

The sea began to rumble. I saw a gold object rise out of the water and come between Ariel and Eric. It was a giant crown! Ariel and Eric were pushed upward as Ursula—a thousand times her normal size—burst through the surface. Ariel and Eric were tiny specks clinging to her giant crown. Ursula's body continued to grow, making a huge shadow that covered the sea. Ariel and

Eric grabbed hands and jumped, splashing into the sea near me.

"You pitiful fools!" the giant Ursula, holding a huge glowing trident, bellowed. "Now I am the ruler of all the ocean! The sea and all its spoils must bow to my powers!"

The sky cracked with lightning. A wave rose between Eric and Ariel, forcing them apart. I was swept up in the wave. Ursula swirled the trident in the sea, and the entire area became a giant whirlpool. Eric was pulled into it, and he spun around and around. Ariel held on to a rock at the bottom of the whirlpool.

The whirlpool was so powerful, it stirred up a shipwreck from the ocean floor. Eric broke out of the whirlpool and swam toward the shipwreck. He grabbed hold and pulled himself aboard.

53

Eric steered the wreck right toward Ursula. The sharp and jagged tip of the broken mast pierced her belly. She let out a terrible cry of pain. Glowing and sizzling, Ursula fell back into the sea and began to sink. Her tentacles lashed out. One of them swiped against the ship, pulling it and Eric underwater.

As I watched, Ursula sank, disappearing forever. Yes! The evil blubber-babe was dead!

I dove back under the water. Ursula's garden of souls was transformed back into mer-people, and King Triton was restored to his former self. His trident had sunk to the ocean floor, and he grabbed it.

The king saw Sebastian and me. The three of us swam up to the surface, where we found Ariel sitting on a rock in the water. She was sadly staring at an unconscious Prince Eric, lying on the beach.

King Triton sighed and raised his trident. "I'm going to miss her," he said, sending a beam of light toward Ariel. Her tail was

transformed
into two
legs, and
suddenly
she was
wearing a
lovely blue
dress. The king
had finally seen how much Ariel loved Eric.

Eric began to move. He sat up and looked around. When he saw Ariel, a smile lit up his face. He ran to Ariel and swept her up in an embrace. I sighed as the prince and Ariel finally shared a long kiss. It was about time!

Ariel and Eric were married in a great wedding ceremony aboard Eric's ship. I watched from the surface of the water with all the merpeople and Ariel's other sea friends.

When it was over, Ariel said good-bye to all of us.

"Thank you," she said, giving me a big kiss. Ariel made me proud that I'd found the

courage to help her fight Ursula. I was going
to miss my best friend. But I knew that Ariel
and Eric would have a very happy life, so
that made me feel a little better.

So, you see, I'm not a scaredy-cat anymore. And no one can call me a guppy,
either. As a matter of fact, I'm kind of famous
with my friends now. They're always saying,
"Tell us that story about how you destroyed
the evil Sea Witch."

Notes:

An Undersea Treasure Has Emerged!

Now on CD-ROM

Ages 5-10

Includes Everything You Need To Build Your Own Books

- Create Your Own Stories
- Conduct An Undersea Orchestra
- Read And Play In An Amazing Story
- Learn Fun Fish Facts
- Design Virtual Aquariums
- Sing Along With Your Favorite Songs
- Play Games And Activities

Create, Learn and Play in A Living World

- Create your own story
- Conduct an undersea orchestra
- Read and play in amazing stories
- Learn fun fish facts
- Design virtual aquariums
- Sing-Along with your favorite songs
- Play games and activities

DISNEY INTERACTIVE

CD-ROM WINDOWS & MACINTOSH

Experience the Magic of
Disney's
THE ❦ LITTLE
MERMAID

Disney's
The Little Mermaid
Book and Doll

A stuffed Sebastian doll and a
paperback edition of the picture
book, *Tales from Under the Sea*
0-7868-4201-6
$16.95
Ages 3-5

Disney's
The Little Mermaid
Chapter Book

Flounder to the Rescue
Full-color illustrations and
free tattoos in every book
0-7868-4139-7
$3.50
Ages 7-9

Disney's
The Little Mermaid
Picture Book

A picture-book retelling, perfect
for Ariel's newest fans
0-7868-4175-3
$4.95
Ages 2-5

Disney's
The Little Mermaid
Junior Novel

Older *Mermaid* fans will love this
junior novelization, illustrated with
eight pages of full-color stills from
the animated film
0-7868-4202-4
$3.50
Ages 8-12

Available at your local bookstore

2 missing pages 11-29-12 ✓